To Tyson,
Our number 1 grandson.
Merry Christmas 2005.
We love you!
Mimi & Papa

To the memory of Florrie.
And for Paul, with love and thanks,
for believing and being there.

First published in the United States 1998 by
Little Tiger Press
N16 W23390 Stoneridge Drive, Waukesha, WI 53188
Originally published in Great Britain 1998 by
Methuen Children's Books, London
Text and illustrations copyright © Jan Fearnley 1998
All rights reserved
Cataloging-in-Publication Data
Fearnley, Jan.
Little Robin's Christmas / Jan Fearnley.   p.   cm.
Summary : Having given away all his warm vests to his cold animal
friends during the week before Christmas, Little Robin receives a
special reward from Santa.
ISBN 1-888444-40-1
[1. Robins–Fiction. 2. Animals–Fiction. 3. Clothing and dress–
Fiction. 4. Christmas–Fiction. 5. Santa Claus–Fiction.]
I. Title.
PZ7.F2965Li   1998   [E]–dc21   98-6895 CIP AC
Printed in Dubai
First American Edition
1 3 5 7 9 10 8 6 4 2

Little Robin's Christmas

Jan Fearnley

It was the week before Christmas,
and Little Robin was getting very excited.
He washed and ironed his seven warm vests,
one for each of the frosty days ahead.

He put on his white vest
and went to skate on the pond.
On the way he met Frog.
"I'm so cold!" said Frog.
"I wish *I* had a warm vest."

Little Robin gave Frog his white vest.
I've still got six vests left, he thought
as Frog thanked him and hopped
off happily.

Six days before Christmas, Little Robin put on
his green vest and dashed out to play in the snow.
Down the path came Hedgehog.
"I'm freezing!" he said miserably.

Little Robin gave Hedgehog his green vest.
I've still got five vests left, he thought,
waving good-bye to his prickly friend.

Five days before Christmas, Little Robin put on
his pink vest and set out to hunt for worms.

He hadn't gone far when Mole appeared.
"Brrrrrrr! The ground's too hard to dig,
and I'm chilly!" he complained.

So Little Robin gave his pink vest to Mole.
It was a bit tight, but Mole loved it.
He was nice and warm.
Four vests left, thought Little Robin.

Four days before Christmas, Little Robin
put on his yellow vest and flew to the
tall oak tree, where he met Squirrel.
"I'm so cold I can't sleep!"
Squirrel said with a yawn.

Little Robin handed over his yellow vest.
Only three vests left now, he thought
as Squirrel thanked him and promptly
dozed off.

Three days before Christmas,
Little Robin put on his blue vest.

He was swooping
down through the clouds
when he saw Rabbit on the hill.
"I'm so cold my teeth are chattering!"
said Rabbit, shivering.

Little Robin gave Rabbit his blue vest.
It made a perfect hat for him.
Well, I've still got two left, he said to himself
as Rabbit went cheerfully on his way.
Two days before Christmas, Little Robin put on
his purple vest and skipped along the riverbank.

Next to the river stood Otter with her baby,
who was very unhappy. "My baby is sick!" she said.

Little Robin's purple vest was just right for
Baby Otter and made him feel much better.
Oh dear, I only have one vest left,
thought Little Robin.

On Christmas Eve, Little Robin
put on his very last vest, a toasty orange one.
He'd been walking and whistling to himself
for some time when he met a cold little mouse
huddled in the garden.

Little Robin felt so sorry for her that he took
off his last wool vest and pulled it over her.
"Thank you!" cried the mouse.

Now it was late. The snow was falling,
and poor Little Robin had nothing to wear.
There was nobody to help him,
and it was a long way back to his nest.
He fluffed up his feathers as best he could
and huddled miserably on a snowy roof.

Soon he fell fast asleep.
Not even the sleigh bells
woke him, or the crunch
of snow under heavy
black boots.

Large hands carefully
scooped Little Robin up.
"You had better come
with me, Little Robin!"
chuckled a gruff,
jolly voice.

The man took him a long way in a sleigh.
When he got home, the man said to his wife,
"This is the generous little fellow I told you about."
"He must have a very special present then," she replied.

And with Little Robin snug and cozy in her lap,
the lady set to work. She pulled a thread from
a big red coat, and with it she knitted a tiny vest.
It was a perfect fit for a little bird.

"I'm very proud of you," said the man to
Little Robin. "You gave away all your
warm vests to other people.
You are full of the spirit of Christmas.

I want you to have this vest.
It is very, very special. It will keep you warm
forever, and when other people see you in it,
it will make them feel warm, too."

It was time to go, and the man put Little Robin
back into his sleigh. Little Robin was very happy.
His chest glowed as red as a reindeer's nose.

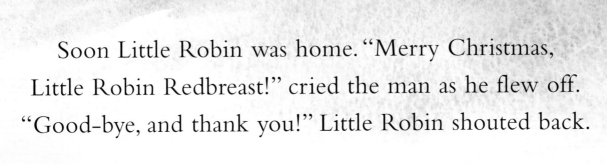

Soon Little Robin was home. "Merry Christmas,
Little Robin Redbreast!" cried the man as he flew off.
"Good-bye, and thank you!" Little Robin shouted back.

It was Christmas morning. Boys and girls
everywhere were opening their presents.
Little Robin flew to the highest branch of a tree,
proudly wearing his new red vest, and sang out
sweetly, wishing everyone a Merry Christmas.